Armin Greder
diamonds

ALLEN&UNWIN

SYDNEY·MELBOURNE·AUCKLAND·LONDON

These are diamonds, aren't they, Mama?

Yes, Carolina, they are.

Diamonds cost a lot, don't they?

Yes, they do.

Did these cost a lot?

I think so.

How much?

I don't know. You'd have to ask Uncle Winston. He bought them for me.

Because he loves you?

Yes, because he loves me very much.

Where did he buy them?

I think in Antwerp, in Belgium.

Is that where diamonds are made?

No, my darling, diamonds are not made, they are mined.

What is mined?

People dig holes into the earth to find things.

If I was to dig a hole in our garden, would I find a diamond?

No, darling, there are no diamonds here.

Where are diamonds, then?

Oh, in other countries. In Africa, for example.

That is where Amina comes from, doesn't she?

Yes, of course.

But Amina isn't rich.

Of course not.

But she has diamonds?

She doesn't have any diamonds!

But you said…

Enough of that now!

Winston is picking me up in a minute.

Amina will put you to bed. Be good.

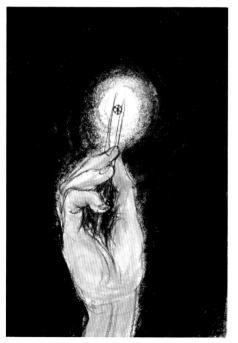

What's going on?
Why is Carolina crying?

Don't worry, madam. It was only a nightmare.

Afterword by Francesco Boille

'Every gun that is made, every warship launched, every rocket fired signifies, in the final sense, a theft from those who hunger and are not fed, those who are cold and are not clothed. This world in arms is not spending money alone. It is spending the sweat of its laborers, the genius of its scientists, the hopes of its children. […] This is not a way of life at all, in any true sense. Under the cloud of threatening war, it is humanity hanging from a cross of iron.'
– **Dwight David Eisenhower**, President of the United States, 16 April 1953

'To those people in the huts and villages of half the globe struggling to break the bonds of mass misery, we pledge our best efforts to help them help themselves […] not because the Communists may be doing it, not because we seek their votes, but because it is right. If a free society cannot help the many who are poor, it cannot save the few who are rich.'
– **John Fitzgerald Kennedy**, President of the United States, inaugural address, 20 January 1961

Armin Greder seems to me to be a truly important writer for understanding these times we live in. And I believe he will become even more important in the future, because once the future arrives – that is, if we survive this senseless moment we are currently living through – the present day will in turn come to be seen as another foolish moment in the past (one of countless such moments …), at least for as long as some notion remains of a possible future for the human race as a whole. And Greder will reveal yet more of his timeless profundity, in books that ought to be jealously preserved in libraries for 'adults' before shifting them into libraries for 'children'. This would be an ideal chain of events, the same chain that seems to be a key element of all his work. In his art, Greder, originally from Switzerland, has pinpointed many of the themes humanity is currently grappling with, or at least that part of humanity that continues to think of others, and indeed of all living creatures. In some of his most significant work, he manages a string of spectacular achievements: brevity, complexity, originality of perspective. And this is because his work is always pervaded by a feeling of 'urgency'.

In this book, Greder's artistic journey seems to have found its clearest expression yet, unless he someday produces a book about global warming that brings together the poor of the rich world with all the rest. (But not only the poor – also the middle class, since the collapse of the middle class is at the centre of the political battle waged by the former 'radical left', who have nowadays transformed into earnest 'new dealers', to borrow the term Noam Chomsky used for his friend Bernie Sanders, such is the regression and reversal of rights that has taken place since the end of the Cold War and the signing of global trade agreements that quickly led to the so-called globalisation of the economy.) His route is linear, direct, but punctuated by constant shifts that are subtle, but definitive. In the afterword to Greder's previous book, *The Mediterranean*, the greatly missed writer and journalist Alessandro Leogrande speaks of a 'double repression' in today's world: 'our denial of the humanity of those who travel by sea, and often die. These voyagers, men and women, are almost never given a name or a surname; it doesn't matter what they look like, what words they speak.' And in fact, as Leogrande so powerfully highlighted, the media communicates to public opinion an image of those people's tragedy that makes them out to be an indistinct, anonymous mass. The second repression – Leogrande continued – relates to the social and economic causes of these desperate journeys. If people pay to make such a journey, it means they are leaving behind something far worse. This is a very important consideration in this moment in history, and not only in Italy, because it demands of us all that we acknowledge both the cruelty and the futility of certain political decisions, given that the desperate will always resume their journey, unless they meet their death along the way. Cruel and barbaric decisions that do not resolve, but rather aggravate, situations that instead call for quite different approaches.

But let's return to Greder, and to what Leogrande wrote about *The Mediterranean*: 'Armin Greder brings these two instances of repression together. He turns them upside down in the story, reminding us of the "food chain" upon which these journeys are founded, the causes and the effects, the faces of the defeated, and those of the sharks.'

That 'food chain', which Leogrande puts in quotation marks, of course, is a poetic-symbolic motif that also appears in this book. This notion has a broad – and deep – meaning, because it is also the chain of humanity 'hanging from a cross of iron', the chain shackling all those undeclared slaves who 'in the huts and villages of half the globe [are] struggling to break the bonds of mass misery'. But if this chain is not broken, if 'a free society cannot help the many who are poor, it cannot save the few who are rich'.

All quite predictable – this is precisely what is happening to us. We are wealthy, but becoming less so every day, though we remain far better off than the poor and very poor of the world's poorest countries, who are pitted against each other by the truly rich and especially by the ultra-rich of the world's richest countries. By the biggest and cruellest 'sharks' – those who, through their pathological addiction to continuous profit, are driving the human race towards mass extinction.

Greder, with his almost entirely visual, and apparently simple, storytelling, masterfully captures the various components that comprise this 'food chain', which is a kind of perversion of the food chains that occur in nature. He calls out our complicity – at times conscious, but very often simply the result of ignorance of the implacable mechanisms of exploitation – in maintaining the chains that keep modern-day slaves … enchained. Whether it is the somewhat less unfortunate, like Amina – the black nanny of the story, whose name seems intentionally to recall that of the author – or the most unfortunate of all, such as those toiling away in Africa's mines and elsewhere in the world.

If Greder's message has multiple threads to it, I now wish to examine at least some aspects of the way he explores it at a formal level. In his drawings of the slaves, a kind of swirl bursts forth from the page, with graphic and pictorial signs combining to form a magma as black as lava, directly emanating from the earth and originating in the most deep-seated human exploitation. These lava-signs are as viscous as they are coarse, meticulously planned yet at the same time spontaneous, at once prickly and soft. Greder is also careful to let the images, the panels, the sequences, breathe. This is a golden rule of comics, even in the apparently illustrative work of masters like Sergio Toppi or Dino Battaglia. Greder works through graphic subtraction, by setting figures against a backdrop of white.

There are also many influences that he himself acknowledges, and one that must surely be highlighted here is Goya and his *Black Paintings*. In those works, the Spanish master manages to find colour in darkness, sliding between black and brown. Greder blends, *melds* this style with that of Honoré Daumier. In fact, certain of Daumier's paintings (*The Drinkers*, *The Burden*) remind us that the master of caricature would have loved the liquid, almost airy style that appears to have driven Greder to elaborate in his own way also upon the work of the German painter Käthe Kollwitz. Though less well known than the other two artists mentioned, her work is greatly esteemed by Greder. But contrary to what one might think looking at the opaque style used in this book and in *The Mediterranean*, Greder also excels at expressive stylisation of faces, as demonstrated by the extraordinary depiction in *The Island* of the frightened yet also threatening islanders who brandish giant pitchforks when they set eyes on a foreigner.

In fact, *Diamonds* is the continuation and a necessary expansion upon themes Greder has been exploring throughout recent years. There is the wall that looms in the prescient *The Island* (2007) and again in *Gli Stranieri* (*The Foreigners*, 2012), a work exploring, among other things, the Israel–Palestine conflict. There is the risk our society will collapse and our species as a whole will become extinct due to our senseless inability to manage our relationship with the planet, a theme that lies at the centre of the dystopian *Lemming* (2016), based on a Richard Matheson story. And finally, there are those hopeless migrations over the sea depicted in *The Mediterranean* (2017). Not to mention the focus on Australia in *Australia to Z* (2016).

Greder is sending an important message in his exploration of these themes. Pessimistic, but important. In the void, the deafening silence – an over-used phrase that is nevertheless more apt than ever at this time in history – created by slogans and grand political projects, which are at least as worthy as, if not better than, those of the Sixties, what remains are individual acts of regular people. People like Greta Thunberg. And artists, including lesser-known ones like Armin Greder. It is this void, this huge, ridiculous blank space of politics, this emptiness, that Greder highlights so well. He uses his art to bring out, subtract, extract. In a world in which borders become ever harder, and walls, albeit illusory ones, are constantly being erected, Greder uses poetry, that perennial political – and moral – weapon, to cross borders, to go beyond.

Francesco Boille is a journalist and film and comics critic. He has written for *Rolling Stone*, *FilmTV* and *Lo Straniero*, and contributes to the film website filmidee.it. He writes a weekly column for *Internazionale*.

Afterword by Riccardo Noury

An adverb of time connects diamonds with their mining: *forever*.

The advertising slogan 'A diamond is forever' is famous, and it no doubt made the fortune of the advertising agency who came up with it.

In this case, the adverb refers not only to the durability of the product, but also and above all to the idea of an eternal connection between the giver and the receiver.

Much less widely known is the fact that the lives of the people who mine diamonds can be ruined forever: due to the danger and precariousness of makeshift mines, the tender age of those who descend into them, and the dust they inhale, which sticks like a coating to the inside of their lungs.

Diamonds come at a high price for those who purchase them and an unbearably high, at times lethal, price for those who mine them.

To gain control of what lies underground, armed militias and regular armies – people above ground, in other words – wage devastating wars. The relationship between the wealth below and the poverty on the surface is incredible.

The Democratic Republic of the Congo is the most glaring example of all this. But elsewhere, in Africa and beyond, diamonds have financed wars, and been exchanged for weapons. That is what lies at the heart of Carolina's nightmare.

As soon as a boy or girl staggers back up to the surface, the supply chain begins: it is made up of unscrupulous profiteers, each taking a cut of the proceeds. This chain ends, in Europe or elsewhere, at the precise moment when an uninformed purchaser chooses a diamond as a gift.

Human rights organisations have for some time now been engaged in a campaign with a dual purpose: raising awareness among consumers so that they make ethical purchases and demand guarantees about a diamond's provenance, and putting pressure on the supply chain so that the origin of every single diamond can be certified 'conflict-free'.

The second goal is difficult to achieve: not only because of the unusually complex processing diamonds require, but also because producers, intermediaries and states have no desire to undergo inspections. The self-certification and voluntary commitments that have led to the so-called 'Kimberley Process' – a certification agreement that aims to reduce the flow of diamonds used to finance conflict – is not enough.

Riccardo Noury is spokesperson for Amnesty International Italy.

A orecchio acerbo.
Non solo pubblicano libri, ma li ispirano.
– AG

First published by Allen & Unwin in 2020

Allen & Unwin
83 Alexander Street
Crows Nest NSW 2065
Australia
Phone: (61 2) 8425 0100
Email: info@allenandunwin.com
Web: www.allenandunwin.com

A catalogue record for this book is available from the National Library of Australia

ISBN 978 1 76087 704 0

For teaching resources, explore www.allenandunwin.com/resources/for-teachers

Illustration technique: compressed charcoal and pastel on paper
English translation of Francesco Boille's and Riccardo Noury's afterwords by Brigid Maher
This book was printed by Tien Wah Press, Malaysia, in March 2020.

10 9 8 7 6 5 4 3 2 1